Luke's jaw dropped down to his knees when he realized a gangling, galloping goalkeeper was charging upfield to join in the fun. The Zebras could not believe their eyes either. The bright, multi-coloured top stood out clearly from the other shirts and their defensive organization fell apart. Nobody knew who was to mark him.

'Get back, Sanjay, get back!' Luke screamed, glancing fearfully at the Swifts' empty goal. 'What are you doing here? Have you gone mad?'

It was too late. Brain whipped the corner over, curling the ball in towards the near post. Sanjay timed his arrival perfectly and barely had to jump. He brushed past an uncertain challenger and sent a bullet header screaming over the full-back who was guarding the line . . .

·ALL GOALIES ARE CRAZY...

...BUT SOME GOALIES ARE MORE CRAZY THAN OTHERS!

ROB CHILDS
ALL GOALIES ARE CRAZY

... BUT SOME GOALIES ARE MORE CRAZY THAN OTHERS!

ILLUSTRATED BY
AIDAN POTTS

CORGI YEARLING BOOKS

ALL GOALIES ARE CRAZY
A CORGI YEARLING BOOK : 0 440 86350 3

First publication in Great Britain

PRINTING HISTORY
Corgi Yearling edition published 1996
Reprinted 1997, 1998

Set in 12/15pt Linotype Century Schoolbook by
Phoenix Typesetting, Ilkley, West Yorkshire

Corgi Yearling Books are published by Transworld Publishers Ltd,
61–63 Uxbridge Road, London W5 5SA,
in Australia by Transworld Publishers (Australia) Pty Ltd,
15–25 Helles Avenue, Moorebank, NSW 2170
and in New Zealand by Transworld Publishers (NZ) Ltd,
3 William Pickering Drive, Albany, Auckland.

Printed and bound in Great Britain by
Cox & Wyman Ltd, Reading, Berkshire.

Especially for all crazy goalies – like me!

1 The One and Only

It looked a certain goal. The ball swerved and dipped as it flew towards the target, an inviting expanse of unguarded netting.

Matthew, the school team captain, let out a groan of dismay, angry at himself for failing to block the shot. Nothing could stop it going in now. Suddenly, a blur of bright colours flashed across his line of sight, deflecting the speeding missile at the last possible moment up and over the crossbar to safety.

'Sanjay!' Matthew cried out. 'Where did you come from?'

The gangly goalkeeper sprawled on the ground, his grin almost as wide as the goal itself. Sanjay lay like that for several seconds, as if posing for a posse of photographers, before springing up onto his feet. 'No sweat!' he smirked, tugging his crumpled, multi-coloured top back into position. 'You know you can always rely on me.'

'Huh!' the captain grunted, hands on hips. 'That'll be the day. If you hadn't fumbled their first effort, they wouldn't even have had another chance to score.'

'Saved it, didn't I?'

Matthew could hardly argue with that. The applause from the smattering of spectators was still continuing and Sanjay soaked it all up.

'Dead brill save, Sanjay!' yelped an excited voice. It came from behind a bobbing camcorder rapidly heading towards them around the pitch.

None of the home players needed to guess who was trying to film and talk at the same time. Everyone in Year 8 of Swillsby Comprehensive knew the sound and sight of soccer-mad Luke Crawford. In fact, most of the pupils in other year groups had heard of him too.

'Keep out of the way, Loony Luke,' Matthew warned him. 'We don't want you here putting us off with that thing.'

Luke's thin, flushed face appeared round the camera, looking hurt. 'Only trying to help, recording the game so you can see what went wrong.'

Matthew scowled. 'Nothing's gone wrong, thanks very much. At least not until you turned up. It's still nil–nil.'

'Won't be for long, if you don't watch out,' Luke replied cheekily. 'They're taking the corner.'

The captain whirled round. 'C'mon, men, mark up!' he shouted.

11

Too late. The ball was whipped low across the penalty area straight to an unmarked attacker lurking just outside the six-yard box. He hit it first time before any of the defenders could react, but Sanjay's reflexes were sharper. He flung himself instinctively towards the danger and the ball smacked him full in the face, his hands unable to parry it.

The goalkeeper had done his duty. He had successfully protected his goal once more, but it was a little while before the game could go on. Sanjay needed some running repairs.

'Frosty' Winter, Swillsby's long-suffering sports teacher and short-sighted referee, cleaned up the boy's bloodied nose with a sponge of cold water. 'There, as handsome as ever!' he lied.

'What a hero!' laughed Adam, the centre-back. 'But try and catch it in your mouth next time, will you? You've given away another corner!'

Sanjay attempted a grin, but it was a bit too sore. He gingerly ran his tongue around his teeth to check they were all present and correct.

'Do you want to carry on?' asked Frosty.

Sanjay looked at the teacher as if it was the most stupid question he had ever heard. 'Sure. Just a bang in the face, that's all. I'm OK.'

Frosty shook his head. 'Must be true, that old saying.'

'What's that, sir?' asked Sanjay, half-guessing what was coming.

'All goalies are crazy!'

'They have to be,' Matthew sneered, 'the way they risk getting their fingers broken, head smashed in and teeth kicked out every match.'

Luke put down the camcorder to fetch the water bucket off the pitch and show his support for his pal's bravery. Sanjay also played for Swillsby Swifts, Luke's lowly Sunday League team. 'Great stuff, Sanjay. You're the best keeper we've got.'

Matthew pulled a face. 'He's the *only* one. Nobody else in the squad is crazy enough to want to play in that position.'

Sanjay knew that the captain wasn't exactly his greatest fan. 'Guess that makes me the best, then, doesn't it?' he replied wryly.

Thanks to more saves from Sanjay, missed chances and good defending by both sides, the

match remained goal-less until soon after half-time.

That was the moment when Jon Crawford, Luke's talented cousin, chose to display his silky-smooth skills. Receiving the ball wide on the left, he shaped to turn one way but floated past his bemused marker the other. Jon glanced up to see the keeper straying off his line and curled a shot with the inside of his right foot tantalisingly over the poor lad's outstretched, groping fingers. An exquisite goal.

Luke could not have done it better himself. In fact, he could not have done anything like it at all, if he had tried for a hundred years. Instead, perhaps recognizing his own limitations as a footballer, Luke did the next best thing. He acted out his fantasy of being a budding sports reporter and live commentator, feverishly describing the drama in words for his imagined nationwide audience as he filmed the action.

'*Jon Crawford, Swillsby's Johan Cruyff, the flying Dutchman, sells a sensational dummy to make the defender look a fool. Jon now moves inside, creating space for a pop at goal, picks his spot and shoots. It looks good – it is good – GOOOAAALLL! Jon Crawford has done it again . . .*'

'Who is this Joanne Cruyff you're always raving about?'

The sudden demand startled Luke enough to interrupt his commentary. He looked around in disgust at the questioner. It was Tubs, slouching, hands in pockets, on the touchline. He was another Swifts' player who, like most of them, could not claim a regular place in the school side.

'It's not Joanne, it's pronounced Yo-han,' Luke corrected him sternly, cross that his hero had been maligned through ignorance or deliberate cheek. Probably the latter, he realized, coming from Tubs.

'Yo, man!' Tubs grinned.

Luke wasn't amused. '*Yohan*, but spelt with a J,' he stressed. 'It's Dutch, see, and – since you ask – Johan Cruyff was the finest footballer ever to grace the turf of the world's biggest and best soccer stadiums!'

'OK, OK, save the poetry for your match reports,' laughed Tubs. 'You reckon Jon plays a bit like him, do you?'

Luke shrugged, just like his laid-back cousin might have done. 'Sometimes, when he's in the mood.'

'Yeah, that's his trouble. Magic one moment

and then disappears from view like the Invisible Man.'

'He can win his team the game in that one moment, though,' Luke defended him. 'Just like he has done today.'

'I shouldn't bank on it,' Tubs said, pointing down the other end. 'Look, they've broken clean through our defence straight from the kick-off. They're going to equalize.'

'Not with Sanjay playing like he is . . .' Luke began. 'Oops!'

The attacker had mis-hit his shot, sending the ball skidding along the ground. Sanjay appeared to have it covered comfortably, but somehow let the ball slip through his hands and into the net.

'I don't believe it!' cried Luke. He knew the keeper had his good and bad days, but this had seemed to be one of his better ones. Luke took his disappointment out on Tubs. 'I've missed that goal now, thanks to you keeping me here talking. We haven't got it on tape to study later.'

Tubs let loose his loud, rumbling laugh. 'I reckon Sanjay will thank me as well when he finds out. He won't have wanted to see that again.'

Sanjay was too busy trying to make his

18

apologies to worry about action replays. 'Sorry, you guys. The ball bobbled up just in front of me.'

'You mean you took your eye off it,' Matthew complained. 'Typical! You've just gone and wasted all our hard work to take the lead.'

'Lay off him, Matt,' Jon interrupted. 'If it wasn't for Sanjay, we'd have been getting slaughtered by now.'

'He's just cancelled out your goal. Aren't you bothered?'

Jon shrugged casually. 'Well, guess we'll just

have to go and score another one, won't we?'

Sadly, it wasn't to be quite that simple. Growing in confidence, the visitors laid siege to Sanjay's crowded penalty area and Swillsby barely even managed another decent attempt on goal, never mind score. They were struggling to hold on for a draw, hoping Frosty would blow the final whistle to rescue them.

'How much longer, sir?' panted Matthew.

'You'll find out soon enough,' Frosty replied gruffly without checking his watch. 'Just keep your mind on the game.'

Luke, too, was hard at work, beavering away along the touchline. *'Inside the final minute, the ball is once more with Sanjay Mistry, Swillsby's eccentric goalie. He's hoping to use up extra precious seconds, dribbling it out of his area, taunting the opposition to come and make him hurry. The number eleven is taking the bait – Sanjay really ought to be kicking the ball away now . . . Oh, no! He's starting to show off, trying to keep possession over near the touchline, shielding the ball from the winger – he's lost it!'*

Luke dried up in horror. His head jerked up from the camera in time to see the panicking goalkeeper clatter crudely into the winger from

behind in his desperation to regain the ball, but the damage had already been done. The ball was gone and Sanjay was left stranded way out of his goal.

The centre-forward pounced on the loose ball and had the easiest of tasks to slide home the vital second goal. The scorer wheeled away into the arms of his delighted teammates while the Swillsby players stood staring at Sanjay in shock. Some threw themselves to the ground, unable to face up to what had happened.

There was not even time for the game to re-start, and the final three cheers from Matthew were decidedly half-hearted.

'Oh, well,' Sanjay sighed heavily. 'You win some, lose some.'

He was speaking to himself. At least for the moment, nobody was talking to him. But he knew for certain they would all eventually have one or two things to say – and he wasn't looking forward to that very much . . .

2 The Seven Commandments

Luke took his roles as captain, player-manager, chief coach and trainer of Swillsby Swifts very seriously. It was, after all, *his* team – even if the names of his dad and uncle were on the official forms.

At the Swifts' mid-week practice session, he hoped to pass on some useful tips to Sanjay. Since the disasters of the last school match, Luke had been reading up all about goalkeeping from the various coaching manuals that cluttered the shelves of soccer books in his bedroom.

First, though, before leaving the changing cabin to brave the chilly village recreation ground, he wanted words with everybody. 'We've been giving too many goals away, men. We've got to tighten up in defence.'

'Why pick on us, Skipper?' asked Big Ben, their giraffe-necked, bespectacled centre-half. 'The whole team is rubbish, not just us.'

'Yeah, we're bound to let a few in when the opposition pitches camp in our half,' added Mark, his partner at the back. 'I've even seen one goalie bring a book out on the pitch to read 'cos he had nothing else to do.'

'That's not true,' Luke insisted. 'Is it? What was he reading?'

Mark laughed. 'Dunno. Nobody got near enough to him to see.'

'Probably a book on how to overcome loneliness,' Sanjay cackled.

'Not something you'll ever suffer from, is it, playing for the school and the Swifts,' Tubs guffawed.

'I don't mind being kept busy. Gives me plenty of practice and helps me improve,' Sanjay replied and then grinned, realizing why everyone had started laughing. 'Well, anybody can make mistakes.'

'Yeah,' Mark put in, 'but it must take loads of practice to make such good ones all the time.'

Luke felt he was losing control of this team talk. 'Look, forget that now, it's ancient history. And, anyway, we're not rubbish, Big Ben. We're getting better every match.'

'True,' Tubs nodded, as if serious for a moment. 'We're only losing by single figures now, not double!'

Luke took up the point, missing the irony. 'Exactly. Now if we're more organized in defence, we can keep the goals down and maybe even score a few ourselves from counter-attacks on the break.'

Big Ben frowned. 'Have you been reading those coaching books of yours again, Skipper?'

'Actually I've been reading *Animal Farm* by George Orwell.'

There was a groan from Dazza, the Swifts' right winger. 'We're having to study that in English this term. It's all about pigs and stuff.'

'Well, there's a bit more to it than that,' said Luke. 'It's brill. You can learn a lot from it, even though it was published back in 1945.'

'That's over fifty years ago,' gasped Big Ben. 'Now who's talking about ancient history!'

Luke ignored him. 'These animals take over a

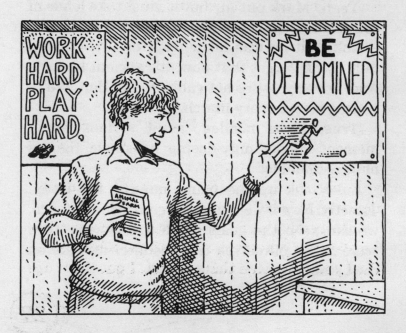

farm, see, led by the pigs because they're the most intelligent . . .'

Tubs interrupted. 'Er, does this have anything to do with football, Skipper? Only I wouldn't mind having the chance to kick a ball about a bit before it gets too dark to see where I'm kicking it.'

'Of course it does, just listen a minute. Snowball showed that . . .'

'Snowball?' queried Mark.

Dazza answered. 'He's one of the pig leaders.'

'Glad to know you're paying some attention in class,' remarked Luke. 'Well, this Snowball was dead clever, full of ideas, and he planned their tactics for when the humans tried to get the farm back. He showed how to turn defence into attack, catch the enemy off guard and pull off a great victory. It was called the *Battle of the Cowshed*!'

The players broke into almost uncontrollable giggles at that and it was a while before they calmed down enough for Mark to speak. 'Has this by any chance, Skipper, got something to do with all these posters that have suddenly appeared in here?'

Luke nodded and smiled with satisfaction as the players' eyes travelled round the cabin walls. 'Glad you've noticed them at last. I put them up

to motivate everybody to do their best.'

'*Be Determined,*' Mark read out the wording on the neatly printed poster above his head, starting the others off.

'*Work Hard, Play Hard,*' Big Ben announced from another.

'*Tactics Win Matches,*' joined in Gary, quickly followed by his identical twin.

'*Teamwork Triumphs,*' Gregg chortled.

'What's this one? *The Referee Is Always Right*!' Tubs snorted. 'Unless it's Frosty, you mean!'

Brain, the Swifts' dyslexic left winger, peered at one poster nearby and shook his head in bemusement. 'There are times like this when I'm quite glad I don't read too well.'

Sanjay did the honours for him. 'It says, *Play To The Final Whistle*. That's worth knowing, eh?'

'Huh! I think I recognize this last one, Skip,' Dazza grunted. '*All Players Are Equal*. That's from *Animal Farm*, right?'

'Dead right,' Luke beamed. 'Snowball put *animals* of course in *his* Seven Commandments, but I reckon it applies to all players in a team too.'

Sanjay grinned. 'Even when one of them is

player-manager – plus captain, coach and any other title he fancies . . . Skipper?'

'Yeah, well,' Luke mumbled. 'I mean, you've got to have some sort of leader, haven't you? The pigs soon made sure the other animals knew that.'

'Was this pig Snowball a good footballer as well?' asked Big Ben.

'Doubt it. Probably a bit too fat, I should think.'

'Like Tubs, you mean?' Sanjay put in, never slow to miss a chance to tease the roly-poly fullback. 'He eats like a pig!'

Tubs took the jibe in good spirit as usual. 'Playing for a team called *Swillsby* Swifts, I reckon it's just as well people nickname us the Sloths instead of the Pigs!'

'What happened to Snowball in the end?' asked Mark.

'That was sad,' sighed Luke. 'The rival pigs got too jealous of him and drove him away.'

'I wonder why?' Tubs remarked drily. 'Perhaps they got fed up listening to him going on and on all the time . . .'

The Swifts were rescued by Luke's Uncle Ray who threw open the cabin door. 'C'mon, get

cracking, lads. I haven't been blowing up all these footballs for nothing. Let's see some action round here.'

Luke took the hint. He quickly organized a training game for most of the squad where the attackers worked to find ways of breaking down the defence. With defenders like the Swifts had, that wasn't too difficult. The hardest part for the equally inept attackers was getting their own shots on target. There was scarcely any need for a goalkeeper 'and Luke left his dad to stand between the posts and supervise the session.

Luke had other plans for Sanjay. He took him down to the far end of the pitch with the Garner twins in order to give the erratic keeper some extra individual coaching. Gary and Gregg began hitting a string of centres high and low into the goalmouth for Sanjay to come off his line and try to gather them cleanly.

'C'mon, Dracula, grab hold of this one,' shouted Gary, as he swept the ball into the goalmouth at catchable height.

Sanjay made a mess of it. He timed his jump well, but totally missed the ball. It sailed between his flailing hands and would have given any attacker behind him a simple headed goal.

Luke sighed as Sanjay pretended to look for holes in his luminous green, goalie gloves. 'Not heard him called that before. Why Dracula?'

"Cos he hates crosses!' Gregg laughed. 'We just made it up!'

'Ha, ha, very funny,' Luke groaned. 'C'mon, Sanjay, never mind those two idiots. Eyes on the ball and keep those hands together. Get them right behind it.'

'Think you can do any better, Skipper?' he asked sarcastically. 'Want to demonstrate how it's done?'

'No, I'm just encouraging you, that's all.'

'Well, don't. I do things my own way, right?'

'You certainly do,' muttered Luke under his breath, but Sanjay caught it – about the only thing he had caught so far.

'What did you say?'

Luke thought quickly. 'I just said, "I'll leave it to you", OK?'

'Hmm . . .' Sanjay murmured, not amused. He loved his goalkeeping and was getting a bit narked by all the recent criticism. 'You'd better do as well. Just don't start interfering.'

Luke had brought along some mathematical charts he'd produced on his home computer to

he's had a little reminder who the real boss is!'

Luke arrived early at the cabin before the Swifts' mid-week practice, making sure that no-one saw him pin up an extra poster. As the players were changing, they kept glancing quizzically at the wall.

Dazza had finished Orwell's story in English and nudged Sanjay with his elbow. 'Seen that?'

Underneath the statement 'All Players Are Equal' was now the pointed amendment: 'But Some Players Are More Equal Than Others'.

Luke could not help feeling a certain pang of jealousy as he stood back and watched Sanjay toss the coin with the Ashton captain. But at least his tactic seemed to have worked.

During the practice session he had smoothed Sanjay's ruffled feathers and the goalkeeper, pride restored, was quick to accept the honour of captaincy. Luke had never seen the normally laid-back Sanjay so keyed up to do well as he was now. He may have been fooling around with all his old mates before the match as they inspected the dried-out Swillsby pitch, but Sanjay also had a steely glint of determination in his eyes. He was out to prove to everybody that he was still the number one.

'Change round, team,' Sanjay called out. 'I've won the toss. I want the wind behind us second half.'

Ashton seemed equally positive. Nothing was going to please them more than defeating the Swifts and putting plenty of goals past their former keeper into the bargain. 'C'mon, the Reds!' cried their captain, Daniel. 'We've only got Sanjay to beat. And you know how easy that is.'

They set out the way they meant to carry on, cutting ruthlessly through the Swifts' porous

defence like an electric saw through a mound of jelly. But inside the wobbly dessert, they found a hard nut to crack – Sanjay.

The goalkeeper was inspired. Whatever Ashton Athletic threw at him, he caught it, punched it, blocked it, dived on it and smothered it – and threw it back at them to try again. Once he even headed a shot off the line.

'Look, Daniel, no hands!' he laughed. 'That's how *easy* it is!'

Luke was also in full flow, at least with his babbling commentary. The words gushed out of him like water from a burst pipe: '*A massive kick from Sanjay, having the game of his life, finds Brain free on the left wing. He holds the ball, relieving the pressure for a time, and then switches play across the field to Dazza on the right. The long pass has caught Ashton flat-footed, but Dazza still needs help. It's offered by the player-manager, Luke Crawford, always on hand to provide support . . . Uughh!*'

Luke was up-ended unceremoniously from behind. Not because he was in a dangerous position, but more because his marker could not bear to listen any longer to his biased commentary. The foul had the desired effect to some

degree, silencing Luke briefly, but the free-kick was not so merciful. Titch took it smartly while Luke was still limping about, Gregg shot and the rebound was rifled home by Dazza from an acute angle.

While the visitors were recovering from that unexpected setback, the Swifts scored again, Gregg himself this time polishing off a move started by Dazza. The 2–0 lead was a travesty of justice and it only served to make Ashton re-double their efforts to put the record straight. By half-time, the scoreline told a different, fairer story.

Despite all his heroics, Sanjay could do little to prevent the first two goals that finally found his net, one high, one low, but both into unreachable corners. And when the third came as a result of a frantic goalmouth scramble, in which the keeper-captain twice excelled himself with brave stops, the Swifts' woes were complete. Sanjay was injured.

Attempting to claw the ball back from going over the line, the goalkeeper had his fingers crushed accidentally under a player's boot. Friend or foe, it wasn't clear, but the damage was just the same.

'There's no way you can carry on in goal,' Luke's uncle said at half-time, which fortunately came soon after the incident. 'My advice is that you go straight home and get that right hand seen to properly.'

'What, and miss the rest of the match?' gasped Sanjay, clearly in pain but not willing to admit how much. 'Forget it! I'm staying.'

'But you can't keep goal like that.'

'I'll play out on the pitch then. I'm not coming off.'

'What do you think, Luke?' asked Uncle Ray.

Luke didn't have a chance to reply. 'He's not skipper today, I am,' Sanjay said defiantly. 'So I decide what we do, right?'

Luke was tempted to quash that by saying he was still player-manager, but wisely bit his lip. 'So who goes in goal?' he asked simply.

'You do!' stated Sanjay. 'Anybody got any objections to Luke playing in goal?'

One or two almost spoke up, but recognized the mood was in Luke's favour and kept quiet. Big Ben voiced the majority feeling of the team. 'Luke's been practising at least. He knows what to do.'

Whether he could actually do it or not was

another matter, but any doubts were not expressed. Luke felt chuffed that he hadn't even had to volunteer or insist he went in goal. The others wanted him to, and that was the important difference.

Sanjay's goalie top came down to Luke's knees and he hastily stuffed it into his shorts before donning the gloves. They were too big as well, but he'd left his own at home.

'Right, men,' Luke said while Sanjay's head disappeared inside the number nine shirt. 'We may have gone and thrown away a two-goal lead, but we don't intend to lose this game. C'mon, let's go out there now and win it for Sanjay!'

8 Seven-a-Side

It was the most mad-cap, see-saw second half. The two sides slugged it out tirelessly, trading goals like swapping football stickers.

The Swifts opened the scoring at both ends. Gregg gave his team the ideal start by putting them back on level terms in their very first attack, blasting home a neat pass from Sean. But this was quickly cancelled out by Luke's second too – his second own goal in consecutive games. And this time he needed no help from the referee. It was all his own work.

Not trusting his kicking after the Frosty business, Luke decided to throw the ball out whenever he could. That was safer – or should have been. In Sanjay's large goalie gloves, however, his grip on the ball was not very secure. As he leant back to hurl it out to the wing, he lost control of the ball and it popped out of his right glove and rolled agonisingly over the goal-line before Luke could react.

'And he talks about throwing things away!' said Sean, shaking his head.

Luke threw the gloves away, too. He tossed them into the back of the net in disgust, preferring to rely on his bare hands. It was to no avail. Soon Ashton went 5–3 up as Daniel slid a low cross past a motionless Luke, still brooding over his gaffe.

The two captains briefly stood side-by-side before the re-start. 'Who's that dummy you've put in goal?' smirked Daniel. 'Has he been bribed to make sure you lose?'

Sanjay sighed. 'No need, he always does that anyway! He's the crazy guy I've told you about before, Luke Crawford. He runs this team.'

'Him!' scoffed Daniel. 'No wonder you're bottom of the league! With him in goal and you out on the pitch, we're going to run riot!'

'Don't count your chickens, you've not won yet,'

Sanjay retorted, just for the sake of it. He didn't even believe it himself. His dreams of a great victory over his former teammates had already been dashed.

At that point, the game might have gone away from the Swifts completely if Ashton had been allowed to score again – and this looked probable when an attacker burst clear through the middle of the Swifts' defence.

Their inexperienced keeper ventured out unsteadily to meet the oncoming opponent, trying to recall the advice in chapter three of *The Art and Craft of Goalkeeping*. Luke didn't want to commit himself too soon, staying on his feet until the last second and narrowing the shooting angle with every metre. The striker was forced to make the first move and the moment he did, intending to dribble round the keeper, Luke pounced and dived at his feet. Amazingly, he won the ball, gripping it tightly to his chest, but was badly winded too when the other boy fell heavily on top of him.

The referee halted the game while Luke recovered his breath, but he refused to let go of the ball. He'd got it and he meant to keep it, relishing the praise from his teammates.

'Blinding save, Skip!' cried Dazza.

Even Sanjay was impressed. 'Good job you brought your protractor to work out all those angles,' he joked.

Then it was Sanjay's turn to bask in the glory limelight. The Draper–Mistry double act worked its magic once more, only this time Brain floated his corner right across the six-yard box for Sanjay's long legs to propel him high above his challengers. He met the ball square on his forehead to power it into the same net he had fought so hard earlier to keep it out of.

Sanjay was overjoyed to score against his old pals, a reward that made him forget all about the tingling ache in his mangled fingers. He played a key part in the next goal, too, brought down outside the area in the defender's anxiety that Sanjay shouldn't be allowed to grab another. Brain did the rest, drilling the direct free-kick with deadly accuracy through the ramshackle wall of bodies and past the unsighted goal-keeper.

'What's the score, ref?' asked Sanjay. 'I've lost count.'

'Five–all, son – I think,' he replied uncertainly.

A little later, the official had to revise his calculations. The Swifts nosed ahead again, with Gregg notching their third successive goal and completing his personal hat-trick at the same time. He was set up unselfishly by his elder twin, who presented him with a simple tap-in goal when Gary himself might well have been tempted to add his own name to the ever-expanding scoresheet.

'Great stuff, I'm proud of you, junior!' yelled Gary into his ear as they celebrated together. He liked to remind Gregg every now and again that

he was ten minutes older and knew how using the term junior irritated his younger brother. It helped to keep Gregg in his place and stopped him from getting too big for his boots!

The Swifts had to be aware of the danger of falling into the same trap themselves. With so narrow a lead, this was no time for a display of over-confidence and Luke should have known better. After making a save, he went and spoiled his good work with a silly piece of bravado. He allowed his enthusiasm and excitement to run away with him, dropping the ball at his feet and dribbling it well beyond his area as if he were still playing out on the pitch. He hoped to be able to kick it further upfield and produce another goal, which it did, but not for the Swifts.

Luke had already seen Sanjay caught out, attempting something similar in the school game, but it didn't stop him repeating the error. Daniel put him under pressure, whipped the ball off his toes and lobbed it towards the vacant goal. Luke was the only player near enough to try and prevent a further humiliation and he hared after the bouncing ball at top speed.

His relief was enormous as the ball struck the post, but it rebounded towards him and Luke

was going too fast to get out of the way. He tried to jump over it but the ball hit his knee and bobbled back into the goal. Luke keeled over and finished up nursing the ball, upside-down, helplessly tangled in the netting by his studs.

'I don't believe it,' he groaned softly. 'Another stupid own goal!'

With only about five minutes remaining, both teams might have been happy to settle for a high-scoring draw, but the match had more stings left in its scorpion's tail.

Tubs was the next in line for match-winning, hero status with his first goal of the season, thumping a long-distance shot high into the roof

of the net. Sadly, the Swifts' delirious cele-
brations that followed were premature. Sanjay
was still to have a hand in the final outcome.

In their desperation not to lose, Ashton
pushed everybody forward in search of yet
another equalizer. In consequence, Swifts pulled
everybody back to try and hold them at bay and
protect their slender advantage. During a fren-
zied attack, perhaps obeying his natural
instincts, Sanjay found himself in his accus-
tomed position on the goal-line. The ball evaded
Luke's grasp and was destined for the net until
Sanjay dived across to his right and knocked it
away.

'Great save!' Mark said, helping Sanjay to his
feet. 'Just a pity you're not actually in goal!'

The referee considered sending Sanjay off for
the handling offence, but felt the boy had suf-
fered enough. He had hurt his bad fingers again
and went to sit down off the pitch behind the goal
in misery. Sanjay could do no more. The result
was now out of his control. The penalty was to be
the last kick of the match.

'It's all up to you, Luke!' he called out.

This was a total new experience for Luke. He
didn't much fancy his chances of saving Daniel's

penalty by normal methods. He decided on the spur of the moment to adopt Sanjay's previously successful tactics instead.

It had helped to bring the Swifts victory before and Luke reasoned that the same high-risk strategy might do so again. He stood poised by the side of the post and then began swaying, wanting Daniel to think he was going to hurtle across the goal.

'No, don't try that!' Sanjay cried in alarm. 'It won't work again.'

'Huh! Bet he doesn't want me to show I can do it too,' Luke grunted. 'With a bit of luck, Daniel will fall for it just like that other kid.'

Luke wasn't to know it , but he was going to need a lot of luck . . .

At the referee's signal, the Ashton captain ran in, ignoring the keeper's antics. He concentrated all his attention on placing the ball into the wide open space and struck it with the inside of his right boot. Bang on target. The kick was tucked into the far corner of the net and Luke never even moved. His mouth dropped open. Daniel hadn't followed the script. He was supposed to hit the penalty straight at him!

'Sorry, Skipper,' came the lame apology from

behind the goal. 'Me and my big mouth! I'd already bragged to him about that penalty stunt I pulled off against the Zebras.'

'You'd done what?' Luke gasped. 'Now you tell me!'

'I was trying to before, but . . .' Sanjay shrugged and started to titter. He couldn't help himself, and soon his infectious giggling spread to the other players, too, as they all caught on to the joke. Even Luke saw the funny side of what had just happened and joined in the laughter.

As the teams shook hands, the referee went over to the touchline. 'Do you make that seven

goals each?' he asked hopefully.

'Aye, a fair result,' agreed Ashton's manager. 'Nobody deserved to lose a roller-coaster of a match like that!'

'Nobody deserved to win it either,' Luke's dad chuckled. 'I reckon both teams were as bad as each other!'

Sanjay hung back in the changing cabin afterwards, taking his time and refusing any help in dressing with his sore fingers. He wanted to be the last to leave and waited until Luke had stepped outside to talk to his dad and uncle.

Sanjay checked through the doorway to make sure he was not going to be disturbed. Then he took out a thick black marker pen from his coat pocket and went up to the posters on the wall. He'd planned carefully what he was going to do, even before such manic performances from Luke and himself in the match. He wanted to get his own back for the skipper's recent rivalry and treatment of him.

'Good job my writing hand's OK,' Sanjay smiled. He crossed out four words on one of the posters and neatly printed his alternative choices above. He was just finishing his task as the door creaked open and he whirled round.

'I think we'd best leave it for our teammates to decide which is which, eh, Sanjay!' said Luke, admiring his pal's handiwork, and the two lads grinned at each other.

THE END

ABOUT THE AUTHOR

Rob Childs was born and grew up in Derby. His childhood ambition was to become an England cricketer or footballer – preferably both! – but, after graduating from Leicester University, he went into teaching and taught at primary and high schools in Leicester, where he now lives. Always interested in school sports, he coached school teams and clubs across a range of sports, and ran area representative teams in football, cricket and athletics.

Recognizing a need for sports fiction for young readers, he decided to have a go at writing such stories himself and now has more than thirty books to his name, including the popular *The Big Match* series, published by Young Corgi Books. *All Goalies are Crazy* is the second title in the *Soccer Mad* series.

Rob now combines his writing career with work helping dyslexic students (both adults and children) to overcome their literacy difficulties. Married to Joy, also a writer, Rob has a "lassie" dog called Laddie and is also a keen photographer.

SOCCER MAD
Rob Childs

'This is going to be the match of the century!'

Luke Crawford is crazy about football. A walking encyclopedia of football facts and trivia, he throws his enthusiasm into being captain of the Swillsby Swifts, a Sunday team made up mostly of boys like himself – boys who love playing football but get few chances to play in real matches.

Luke is convinced that good teamwork and plenty of practice can turn his side into winners on the pitch, but he faces a real challenge when the Swifts are drawn to play the Padley Panthers – the league stars – in the first round of the Sunday League Cup . . .

The first title in an action-packed new football series.

0 440 863449

SOCCER AT SANDFORD
Rob Childs

'We're going to have a fantastic season!'

Jeff Thompson is delighted to be picked as captain of Sandford Primary School's football team. With an enthusiastic new teacher and a team full of talent – not least that of loner Gary Clarke, with his flashes of goal-scoring brilliance – he is determined to lead Sandford to success. Their goal is the important League Championship – and their main rivals are Tanby, who they must first meet in a vital Cup-tie . . .

From kick-off to the final whistle, through success and disappointment, penalties and corners, to the final nail-biting matches of the season, follow the action and the excitement as the young footballers of Sandford Primary School learn how to develop their skills and mould together as a real team – a team who are determined to win by playing the best football possible.

0 440 86318 X

SANDFORD ON TOUR
Rob Childs

'We're on our way!' shouted Jeff. 'Let's go! Let's get at 'em!'

The footballers of Sandford Primary School are off on tour! Invited to take part in a major schools football tournament, an exciting six days is planned for the whole first team squad. Not only are they to take part in the tournament itself, but they are to play a couple of friendly matches on the way *and* have a go at a variety of other outdoor activities – including rock-climbing and caving.

It's a great chance for Sandford to show what they can do and Jeff Thompson, captain of the squad, can hardly wait to be off. But when they arrive at the tournament, they run up against the home team Waverley – a team who play as rough as they can get away with. And Waverley issue a challenge – a challenge that Sandford are determined to meet . . .

An action-packed and thrilling footballing tale – from the author of *Soccer at Sandford*.

0 440 863201

THE BIG MATCH
Rob Childs

'ACE SAVE, CHRIS!' shouted Andrew as his younger brother pushed yet another of his best shots round the post. 'You're unbeatable today.'

But will he be unbeatable when he is picked to stand in for the regular school team goalkeeper in a vital cup game against Shenby School, their main rivals? For Chris is several years younger than the rest of the team – and they aren't all as sure of his skill in goal as his older brother is . . .

A fast-moving and realistic footballing story for young readers.

0 552 524514

THE BIG PRIZE
Rob Childs

'Huh! Some lucky mascot you're gonna be – Selworth have got no chance this afternoon with you around!'

Everything seems to be going great for Chris Weston. First he wins the prize of being chosen to be the mascot for the local football league club for their next F.A. Cup match. Then he is picked to play in goal for his school team on the morning of the same day.

But then disaster strikes and Chris can hardly walk, let alone run out on to a pitch. Has his luck suddenly changed for the worse? And will he miss his chance of being a mascot?

A lively and action-packed new title in a popular series about two football-mad brothers.

0 552 528234

HERE WE GO!
Diane Redmond

We stared at him, incredulous. He MUST have got it wrong. We COULDN'T be playing LAST SEASON'S LEAGUE CHAMPIONS . . .

With a headmaster like 'Floppy' Fairweather, a great believer in anti-competitive sports, no-one at Moorside school has ever played much football. They don't even know the rules! But Danny, Tamz, Imran and the other kids who volunteer to make up the school's first ever football team quickly discover just how much fun the game can be. Not only that but they can't wait to get out there, start playing and WIN. Even if their first opponents are last season's league champions . . .

A terrific and fast-paced footballing tale, packed with fun and action, from the very first kick-off to the final whistle of the last vital Cup match of the season.

0 440 863260